The Thunder Maker
and
Adventure in the Amazon

©Suzanne Rothman

Read, think, imagine and you will
grow to be a force of nature

Readers Make Thinkers!

During a Thunderstorm:
Get inside a fully enclosed building
&
Wait 30 minutes after the last clap of
thunder before you go outside

Table Of Contents

Chapter 1
Magical vs Tragical

There are many tales about the thunder.
There are many questions about thunder.
Some believe the sound is treacherous. Others
say the sound is made by wild animals such
as the Howler Monkey or a Yellow Banded
Poison Dart Frog.

You can choose to imagine the thunder as
simply that if you like. After all, the imagination
is a place of endless possibilities. Yet, if you
want to learn the melody of thunder, this will
allow the imagination of endless adventures.

A thunderstorm can be magical or
tragical. It is all determined by your view.
During a thunderstorm, people can create
quite a scene. For years, the thunder made
people cover their ears and run. It made
them scream and raise their fist at the sky.

Sure, at the same time as a
thunderstorm, there are huts that hold
napping babies and snoozing
grandparents. There are huts hosting

leaders who teach the children how to carve a perfect fish hook. A few huts are occupied by builders who construct amazing two-story banana leaf forts; the top half is for clay dolls of course. And there are huts where bakers are pounding fresh picked batches of cocoa beans to enjoy for the evening.

Yet, other huts had more than half the village on the lookout during a storm. Large banana leaves of every shape would be pointed at entrances and exits. If the noise is from the thunder, they shouldn't panic. However, if it's not the thunder - they should hide their precious belongings.

Crafty little imposters called the Thuumps like to echo the sound of thunder. Thuumps love causing din and damage. There is only one thing Thuumps enjoy more - snatching up our goods.

Never fear. There is a mighty princess and she will help capture those pesky Thuumps. Her name is Princess Nahy-tro.

Princess Nahy-tro is a protector and she carries the melody of thunder.

Princess Nahy-tro is from the family of the Lightning Elves and she journeys from their magical home on Titan in the midst of a thunderstorm when a rescue is needed. She travels through the Thunder Maker when trouble is awry. The Thunder Maker is a mysterious passageway filled with endless possibilities and Titan is the largest moon of the planet Saturn. It is the Land of the Lightning Elves. The mystic colors of Titan have earned it the nickname the mermaid moon. However, it does have a smudge on one side. You don't need a map to know that the smudge is the tragical property of the Thuumps. It is known as The Unsung Sand Land.

The Unsung Sand Land

Chapter 2
Exxagerator Braggerator

The forest is one of the greatest gifts. It is full of natural resources. Aline and Kal knew this. They lived in a village right outside the forest.

Imagine if you opened your back door and could hear the roar of the Bengal tiger, the squawk of a macaw, and the hissing of an Emerald Tree Boa. Imagine if you stepped one toe out of your back door and pressed it into the lush forest floor. The damp green moss would look like a sock on your foot. Imagine if you could smell the Giant Water Lilies, The Lobster Claw flowers, and the Monkey Brush vines. Aline and Kal did not have to imagine. Every morning when they yawned and stretched with the sunrise, they soon ventured out into the wild rainforest. The rainforest was their home. The rainforest was their school. The rainforest was their fun.

Aline and Kal are from a family of indigenous people. These families are sometimes called tribes. Their home is in the shape of a large circle called a

Shabonos. Aline's family lived 4 huts down from Kal's family.

The tribes live in a village near a river. The large home they share provides shelter for 300 families! Aline and Kal's ancestors passed down thousands of years of traditions that Aline and Kal still practice today. For example, both Aline and Kal know the difference between poisonous berries and delectable berries. The two of them are experts at plucking the sturdiest and widest banana leaves. Plus, the pair is great at gathering prized wild honey.

These traditions connected all the families in the Shabonos. The families knew each other well and shared these impressive skills. Every one worked together to keep the community home clean and strong. Well, almost everyone... Kal always tried to get out of work. And he was often successful. But you wouldn't know that listening to him or his parents.

When the tribes gathered around the flickering campfire to laugh and share food and stories, Kal's family would swoop in and steal the show. They would interrupt with a story about Kal and how

he did something better. They would stand in the spotlight and preen about how Kal had the finest tools and canoe. Aline knew they exaggerated. For example, not long ago, his parents blared that Kal was a great fisherman. "He caught so many fish, we had to tell him to slow down and save some for others," they laughed.

This irritated Aline, yet she was taught to be respectful and didn't interrupt. It was true that Kal was an excellent fisherman. But he wasn't perfect. No one was.

Aline caught fish near the same spot Kal did. Once she saw Kal catch two scrawny fish. They were the size of the palm of her hand! And she saw the two tiny fish nearly pull Kal right into the river. But this did not stop Kal from strutting around the village, "I have a brand new fishing pole. It's the best one around. I could catch every fish in the river if I wanted."

Aline was simply not a fan of braggery. She vented to her parents, "It's not fair. They talk over everyone and they exaggerate!" Aline crossed her arms.

The center of the Shabonos is a valued spot for cooking, dancing, sharing stories, celebrations and learning.

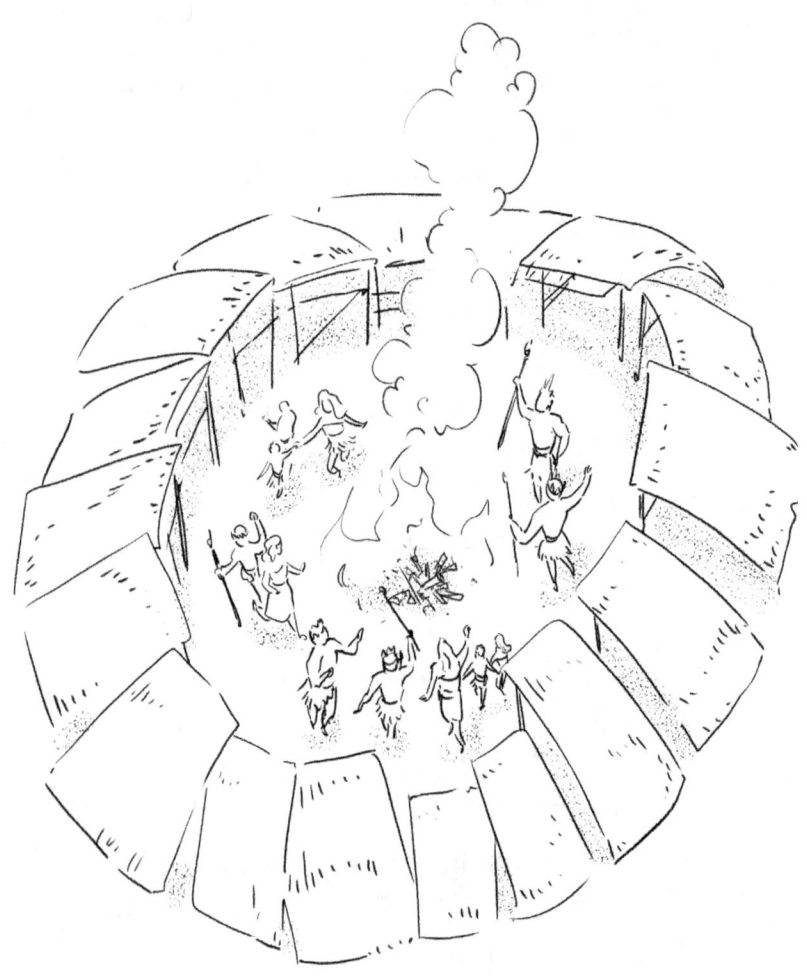

"Calm down, Little One," Aline's father would say.

"You can't stop the Bare-throated Bellbird from singing his song," Aline's mamma would say.

"What does that mean?" Aline asked.

"The Bare-throated Bellbirds call is as loud as the car horn that picks up the harvest. It's honking is so loud it drives other animals away. It makes village children cover their ears."

"That's what I feel like doing," Aline admitted.

"But the Bare-throated Bellbirds do not hear their song as a loud honking horn."

"What does that mean?" Aline asked again.

"It means they are self-absorbed in their song and cannot see all they are moving out of their path."

"Kal and his parents aren't birds, though!"

"True, yet they are a part of the rainforest, Little One. Learn to appreciate them for simply that."

Aline wasn't sure how she would appreciate an exaggerator braggerator.

The rainforest provided a rare and dear way of life. This meant every family had special stories to share. But not when Kal was around. In every story, he was king of the rainforest. And Kal never shared the stage with anybody. Ever. He was louder and more annoying than the Bare-throated Bellbird.

Chapter 3
The Loudest Honk

A big day was approaching. Aline had spent the year preparing for it. She practiced every day for the fun contest known as The Great Games.

The Great Games was only held once a year. It was a contest for the children of the rainforest. The first place winner would win a bundle of prizes including:

⭕a brand new banana leaf hammock

⭕a jug of prized wild honey

⭕they'd be an official announcer at upcoming ceremonies

⭕and best of all, they would hold the championship title for the entire year!

A special crown would be placed atop the champions head. This crown would be full of rare feathers and flowers from deep in the rainforest and was a symbol of great knowledge and love of their home. Aline thought the colors of the crown were remarkable and would make her parents proud. She wanted to honor her parents because they taught her so much about the rainforest.

Also, Aline's mouth watered at the thought of a fresh banana dipped in wild

honey or honey drizzled on sweet corn. She thought of the many recipes she could create with the prize jar of wild honey. You can see why Aline practiced every chance she could.

Aline learned what flowers and plants could be used for medicine. She practiced harvesting unbruised bunches from tall banana plants. She even took a thin clay tablet and charcoal pencil every where she went. On this clay tablet, she drew all the places she visited. Aline was creating her very own map, a map of the rainforest deep within. She marked its surroundings including secret paths, grottos, and lairs. Aline was determined to know every nook and cranny of her dense tropical home.

She knew where the waterfalls were. She knew where the cocoa trees were. She knew that when these trees sprouted white and pink flowers, it meant the ripe pods would soon produce yummy chocolate.

She could take one look at the brown silk on a cornstalk or its green husk and know the sweetcorn was ready to be picked.

However, there is one thing Aline could not know. She didn't know the list

of challenges that would be in the upcoming Great Games. Those tasks would be revealed soon. Still, Aline was all set. She practiced so much that she felt confident about competing except for one small problem. The canoes.

All the indigenous children learned how to row and navigate a canoe. Aline did too. She loved her canoe. Despite that, she was not a fast rower. Sometimes when she practiced, she would look over her shoulder certain that a grey manatee had snuck aboard to weigh down her canoe and make it harder to row. However, that was never the case. The fact was that Aline's arms simply tired quickly from her heavy wooden oars.

Aline knew canoes would have to be a part of The Great Games. This meant she would just have to do her best because using a canoe was the easiest way to navigate the river. It was the number one way of transportation in the rainforest! Now that did not mean that the tribes were unfamiliar with cars. There are a few narrow roads in the rainforest forged by cars for travel. Large cars would visit to

pick up and trade goods with the tribes. The children loved to watch the giant cars roll in like a shiny parade of metal carriages. Each automobile was a dazzling color and each had a different sounding horn. Aline thought for a minute as she compared the three horns in the rainforest. She laughed to herself as she determined who had the loudest honk.

O The Bare-throated Bellbirds
O The large cars
O Kal

Chapter 4
Fast is Not Always First

It was finally the day of The Great Games. Excitement filled the air. Aline barely slept the night before. She could hardly wait to take part in the fun. But, she was able to doze a little and when she did, she had the wildest dreams. She dreamt she was swimming alongside a school of fish. She dreamt that she was racing long-tailed macaws. She dreamt about rowing her canoe so fast that it hovered above the water. And oddly, she dreamt that her canoe turned into a fancy race car zooming over the finish line of The Great Games.

Aline knew that even if all the other children beat her back to shore, they may not be able to catch a full basket of fish. She could.

Fishing was essential to the way of life of the indigenous people, so Aline guessed it would also be part of The Great Games. Fishing was not an easy task, but Aline had a special skill that might help her make up for her slow poke rowing.

Aline dreamt that her canoe
turned into a fancy race car.

She skipped and danced as she got ready for the wonderful day. Not even her slowpoke rowing would cause her to lag. Besides, Aline was certain that Kal would be the first one back to the finish line. Kal rarely ever made the same effort as the other kids. Because he did less work, he often finished first. But, Aline knew that fast is not always first. In order to win, the children would have to carefully complete each task.

All the children arrived in the center of the Shabonos to study the tasks of The Great Games. Children and parents squeezed around to read the list. Aline could already hear loud honking. It wasn't the Bare-throated Bellbird. It wasn't a big car. It was Kal and his parents.

They hogged the spot where The Great Games scroll was posted. Kal's parents had already granted Kal the victory, "Oh Kal, you will race through these tasks! You can pick enough alligator pears to feed the village. Just try to save some for others," they congratulated him and patted him on the back.

Aline jumped up and down over the crowd to get a glimpse. She wished she could soar above the honking to read the scroll. Aline decided to ignore today's honking. She was thrilled to be a part of The Great Games. Once she focused more on what she wanted rather than halting the honking, she made her way to the front of the crowd and read the list herself.

All the tasks were to be completed by sundown.

FILL A BASKET WITH COCOA PODS

FILL A BASKET WITH BANANAS

FILL A BASKET WITH ALLIGATOR PEARS

FILL A JAR WITH WILD HONEY

FILL 2 BASKETS WITH FISH

CROSS THE FINISH LINE BY SUNSET

Aline didn't know that an annoying little bunch of critters was also reading the scroll. The dastardly little bandits known as the Thuumps had rolled into town ready to do the boogey to the loudest, ear-splitting honking they could goad! The Thuumps were always on the lookout to encourage trouble and when they detected a horn in the Amazon, they wanted to seize the opportunity to do more damage. Well, luckily Princess Nahy-tro was also on the lookout and caught wind when five Thuumps escaped from the Unsung Sand Land. How did she spot them you ask? Princess Nahy-tro can see all the way from Titan, so she has no trouble peering right through the treetops in the Amazon.

She was on their tail and perfectly ready to cream those pesky potatoes of destruction. But could Princess Nahy-tro reach the Thuumps before they reached Aline and Kal?

And so the adventure began.

Chapter 5
The Clay Map

The Great Games consisted of five tasks. Four of the tasks represented the four corners of a compass. And these four corners of the rainforest could only be reached by navigating what was smack dab in the center. The river. This meant Aline would have to use her canoe.

"Step away, step away and learn from the best," Kal puffed up his chest and shoulders while blowing his own horn.

"I will fill my baskets the fastest and row with the wind."

"Save some for others," Kal parents were amused by his spunk. "And you will still be the champion!" they whooped.

Aline wanted to cover her ears. The honking gave her a headache. She wasn't jealous. She wasn't mad. But, she was a bit puzzled. How could they gloat about winning when the games hadn't even begun?

Other parents gathered around to offer last bits of support and high-fives to their children. Aline didn't hear her parents at first. She was busy imagining that she was a jaguar.

Aline was pleased, "I believe I can do all of the challenges!"

"I am the fastest! I row with the wind!
All the prizes will be mine!"

Aline daydreamed she was a jaguar who would open her mouth wide to snarl at Kal. She would show her sharp teeth until he jumped back and she wouldn't stop until his parents quieted their loud honking. This made Aline giggle, yet she quickly snapped out of it when her parents called to her again.

"Aline, you do not have time to waste."

"You're right," Aline agreed. She secretly thought to herself that the idea of being a jaguar, for a just a second, was so worth it. Aline scrammed back to her hut to get her map. Just then, the crafty little imposters known as the Thuumps began to echo the sound of thunder. They too were just warming up for the day.

Aline made it back to her canoe in the nick of time. The Great Games were about to begin. All the canoes lined the bank of the river. Aline hopped right into hers as the gleeful call rang out, "Good luck to all!"

Proud parents waved their children off as the sound of thunder in the distant sky rumbled.

Aline's heart stopped for a moment. She already had difficulty rowing the oars of her canoe. What if the rain made the oars heavier and the river choppier? Nonetheless, the children of the rainforest were use to rainfall. Aline wasn't scared of a few sprinkles. However, it was important to her to plan a smart route since the rain might affect the speed of her rowing. She was determined to do her best in The Great Games. So Aline pulled out her map and began to formulate the paths she would take.

Meanwhile, the Thuumps found a new place to do their disco of doom. Those rascally rodents couldn't wait to rock the boat. So where do you think they landed? Five steaming spiky shadows tap danced on Kal's canoe. Yet Kal rowed away so fast, he didn't even notice. He didn't even bother to wave bye to his parents.

5 Thuumps landed to do their disco of doom

Aline didn't see the five holy terrors either. She was studying her map as drops of water sopped on top of it.

Aline counted on her fingers the contest tasks. She needed to reach the cocoa pods, the bananas, alligator pears, the wild honey, and the fish. With her finger, Aline traced a route on the clay tablet. Light droplets of water fell on the map and slid around to help create her path.

Through the corner of her eye, Aline saw many of the children paddling up the river. Aline needed one more minute to concentrate on her plan. She decided she would begin her race in the North. It will be on that corner of the rainforest that she would find the cocoa pods. Along her route, she would catch fish. This would save time since she had to travel the river to reach the four corners of the rainforest.

Aline found a shortcut on her map to the alligator pears in the West. Alligator pears were also known as avocados. After that, she could dash straight across to the East to fill her jar with wild honey. On her way back she would stop for bananas. Then she would race to the finish line.

Aline set her clay tablet on the canoe floor and turned to wave bye to the crowd of parents still watching proudly at the banks. Aline used her oars to push her canoe out to set sail. The sound of thunder roared. Aline could not have known that the claps and booms in the sky were orchestrated by the Thuumps. They were pros at using the ear-piercing clamors to cover their rambunctious behavior.

Chapter 6
Good Luck Spit

Aline pointed her canoe to the North.
The other competitors took off so quickly
that Aline practically had the river to
herself. The canoe ride began calm
despite the recent heavy traffic. Even the
light drizzle was soothing. But, that was
about to change.

A flock of macaws flew overhead just as
Aline arrived in the North. Aline thought
she counted 14 of the vibrant birds, but
quickly turned her attention back to the
first task.

*There are several places to collect
cocoa pods*, Aline thought. Yet, based on
her map, she chose a tree line she drew
just a few days ago. It was easy to reach if
you knew the shortcut off the bank. Aline
saw two other friends in the North, but
they were trekking into the wooded area
with an armful of baskets. Aline turned
her canoe into a shallow part of the bank
and jumped off with her fishing pole and
one basket. Sure enough, she only had to
walk about five steps to find a sprawling
cocoa tree. She grinned with delight when
her eyes landed on a row of blossoming

white and pink flowers. A family of
monkeys perched on the branches of one
of the cocoa trees and they happily
munched on sweet pulp. They stopped
briefly to inspect Aline. The monkeys
quickly returned to their midday snack.
Aline didn't mind the company. Monkeys
meant good luck. Monkeys ate the pink
jam inside the cocoa pods and spit out the
seeds. Aline imagined if she spit out
seeds, her mama would say that was rude.
But when monkeys dribbled out the seeds,
they spread them across the lush
rainforest floor. This helped grow more
cocoa trees. The monkeys had good luck
spit.

Aline looked up at the long, towering row of cocoa trees. She thought they had to be as long as two canoes stacked one on top of the other. She picked out a cocoa tree that did not seem to have any visitors. She dragged her canoe underneath the tree and turned it over. Then she balanced herself on top of her canoe and used her fishing pole to reach the cocoa pods. One by one, Aline knocked off the oval footballs. Into her basket they fell. Aline filled her basket lickety-split, slid off the back of her canoe and reloaded it. She studied her clay map again as warm droplets of rain fell. Her next stop would be in the West where the alligator pears were fully grown.

Maybe I should catch a few fish, Aline thought. She knew of a mini waterfall cliff where fish were plentiful. But according to her map, the waterfall was closer to the South. Aline decided to wait to catch fish until it was time to head South. She couldn't have known that the Thuumps would be waiting too.

With her finger, Aline traced a
route on the clay tablet.

Chapter 7
Avocado Curveball

Aline arrived in the West and to her surprise, many of her friends were already leaving with baskets full of alligator pears. Aline wasn't worried. She was glad for her fellow competitors. After all, what fun was competing if there wasn't any competition?

Aline knew of a tree that produced the sweetest avocados. Even better, she wouldn't need to climb it. This would save time. She waved to her friends and they waved back as they rowed away. Aline parked her canoe near what looked like a thick flower patch. She knew alligator pears were in there. She knew they were a vivid green so they blended in perfectly with the leaves of the trees and they could not be seen from the river bank. Aline had drawn their classified location on her map and she knew exactly which trail to take.

Aline carried her basket to a tree bearing the large green scaly fruit. The alligator pears hung in abundance and their weight pulled the tree branches down. All Aline had to do was snap them off so they fell right into her basket. By the time Aline made her way back to her canoe, alligator pears were spilling over her basket. Just before she placed her overflowing basket into her canoe, something bounced off the top of her head.

"Ouch," Aline cried as she looked around. On the ground next to her was an alligator pear. Aline didn't have time to waste, yet she wanted to know who threw that avocado curveball. Aline walked back to the tree. She didn't see any animals. Nor did she see the five mischievous mud balls tucked inside the trees. Those Thuumps were hiding in the foliage. Each of them held an avocado and they were laughing hysterically.

Aline didn't see anyone nor did she hear the snickering. She couldn't waste another minute. She began to race back to her canoe, but sure enough another avocado zipped past her head. Aline stopped, put her hands on her hips and quietly walked back to find a culprit. Then she heard a noise. The trees were rustling. Uh-oh. Out strutted Kal! And what was he carrying? His arms and hands were full with a huge basket of alligator pears.

Aline was very mad. She was about to confront Kal about the avocado curveballs that hurled past her. If one had hit her hard enough, she might have gone unconscious! Kal would then get the lead in The Great Games. If one had tripped her, Kal could steal her basket of alligator pears. But then, Aline stopped to think. Sure, Kal loved to toot his own horn, yet he was not a real meanie. Aline couldn't imagine that Kal would try to knock her out with an avocado. *No*, Aline thought. *Kal is more annoying than a super loud honking horn, but he is not a crook.* Besides, Aline clearly saw that Kal had his own basket full of alligator pears.

Kal saw Aline staring toward him. He looked around. He looked side to side. He wasn't sure why she had a frown on her face or why her hands were on her hips or why she seemed to be snarling like a jaguar. There were no signs of any other competitors. But then, both in unison, Aline and Kal realized they were losing precious time. Both sprinted to their canoes. The race was on.

Five plump Thuumps still hid in the fruit tree juggling alligator pears in their furry little hands.

5 Thuumps juggled alligator pears

The wind began to pick up speed and the sprinkles of rain began falling harder. An alligator pear hit Aline again, but this time one boomeranged off of Kal too. Neither of them had time to stop. Both of them thought the other threw it. Low and behold, the tricksters in the trees were having a ball causing chaos. Luckily Princess Nahy-tro wasn't far.

Aline rowed away and once she was clear of the embankment, she moved her tangled hair out of her face and picked up her clay map. She slid her finger straight across to the East. She felt relieved. She had completed two tasks and still had plenty of time to cross the finish line. Still,

Aline knew that filling a jar with wild honey was by far the toughest of the tasks. In the meantime, the Thuumps began twirling and doing flips causing the wind to scurry dangerously. This made it difficult for all the competitors to row. If the wind became any more fierce, it would become dangerous for the children competing in the contest.

Aline inserted the blade of her paddle into the river. She crouched low to get a firmer grip on her oars. She saw many children heading North. She didn't know how many more tasks they had to complete, but the storm was escalating. This would surely make the long journey back to the Shabonos more challenging.

Up for the challenge, Aline paddled to the East.

Chapter 8
A Thousand Buzzing Bees

Aline's arms felt like two noodles by the time she drifted into a fork in the river. She had dipped her paddle into the water and out of the water. She twisted at her tummy to use her upper body to get more power in her strokes. Water splashed up her arms as she gained speed. Aline was pretending she had the velocity of a train.

Aline's father told her stories about the Devilish Nose Train. He helped build the train route as a young man and was one of the first passengers on the test ride. He told Aline and her mother tales of how the steam engine raced the wind. He said the air whistle on the train was so loud, it made grown men jump a foot high when the conductor blew it to warn workers to move out of the way.

This is what Aline imagined as she rowed. She lunged forward and pretended her canoe was a shiny express train on the water. And her train would have a louder horn than the Bare-throated Bellbirds or Kal.

The air whistle made grown-ups jump.

Aline could feel droplets of sweat trying to form on her forehead, but the howling wind flicked away her perspiration and replaced it with falling water. She was sore from rotating the oars like they were wheels on a locomotive.

Aline cruised in front of the grassy fork. She knew she was in the right spot. Out in front of her stretched a large Y blanketed in reeds and surrounded by water.

Aline had to choose which canal to take.

Aline pointed to her map. The beehive was logged to the East.

Aline's canoe made ripples in the river as she pulled forward into the hidden cove. She heard the loud sound of the hives even over the winds. All she needed to do was to pick one hive. This was tricky. She couldn't take honey from a thousand buzzing bees. So, she would need to pacify the hive; a trick her mom and dad taught her well. Aline had to hurry. She had already wasted time playing dodgeball with avocados. The storm picked up. Aline lugged her canoe up a footworn lane to a tree with a hive low enough she could reach. She leaned her canoe on the side of the tree to create enough of a barrier from the rain. Aline's first goal was to make the remaining bees flee. To do this, she needed to create smoke using sticks.

Aline used two sticks and the dry leaves her mom packed in the fold of her baskets. She rotated her tired arms then mustered her strength. Aline rubbed the sticks together as fast as she could. This caused friction and formed smoke. Then she lightly tossed on a dash of charcoal that her mom had packed in her dress pocket. The smoke became more pronounced. Now for the tricky part. Aline had to add the smoke to the dry leaves. This would ignite more fumes. Aline gently set the stack of leaves near the once thundering beehive hoping the bees would fly away from the fumes. Once the hive was clear, Aline put on cloth gloves. She placed her hand in the hive and wiggled the honeycomb. She beamed when out popped a huge golden block of honey. It was dripping in gooey sap.

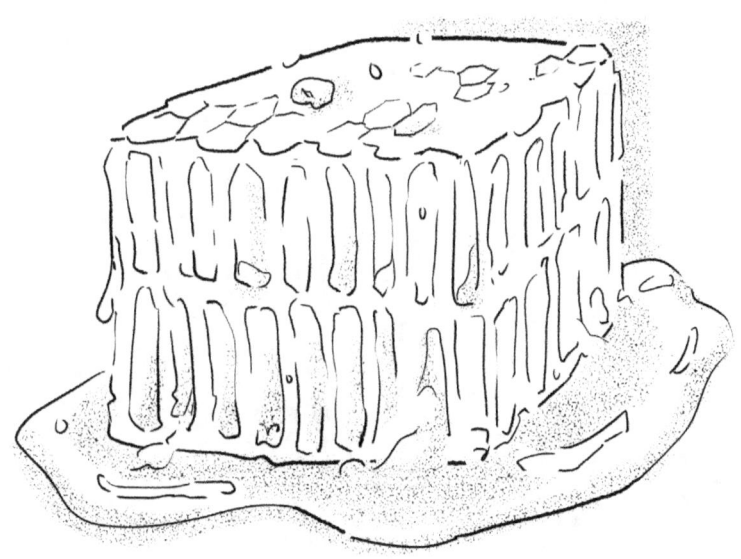

Floral and fruity scents cut through the smokey air around her. Aline was so proud of herself. She knew there was plenty more delicious honey further down, but luckily she only had to fill one jar. The large chunk of honey she collected was enough to fill the jar and allow her a few mouthfuls of the sweet delicacy.

Aline was closer to winning. All she had to do now was catch her fish and grab a basket of bananas. Her heart was racing as she darted South.

Chapter 9
Rock The Boat

Aline stopped midway when she reached the rushing dam where fish filled the river. Water swished over the small rock cliff and the fish dived off as if they were in their own swimming competition.

Tribes learn how to use Bengal bamboo spears to catch fish. But, Aline had her own style of fishing. She made a makeshift crane by sliding her fishing pole into the top of an empty basket. Her pole stuck out of each end of the basket. Then she leaned over the starboard of her narrow canoe and held it out to make a perfect landing spot for the flying fish. They practically jumped in her basket. All Aline had to do was scoop up the fish. Once filled, Aline doubled the baskets and lined them with cloth so water would not escape through the weaves. Aline taught herself to catch many prize dinners using this technique.

Aline raced South toward the finish line. The river was choppy. She knew of many banana trees on this route and didn't need her map. Aline was an expert at harvesting unlike some kids like Kal who felt that wasn't his job. The tribes depended on many things to survive including harvested corn, yucca, tomatoes and of course the alligator pears. The indigenous people shared large gardens and it was everyones responsibility to harvest vegetables and fruits. But, Kal preferred to spend his time practicing with his spear, kicking dirt, or sitting in a banana leaf hammock. He often skipped out on harvesting, yet boasted as if he did as much work as the rest of the children. This made Aline cringe. However, today she was grateful she never tried to get out of work. This made her stronger. She knew she could practically stick her arm our of her canoe and pluck bananas as she rowed. She was on her way to victory.

Then out of the blue, Aline heard what sounded like a loud air horn. It trumpeted like a Bare-throated Bellbird in distress. Through the grey haze of the rain, she saw a canoe bouncing up and down on the rough waters. There didn't seem to be anyone in the canoe. The wind was sharp and zigzagged around her, spraying water in her face. Aline could not see the five fizzling shadows conducting a ballet dance around the deck of a canoe. Aline heard a loud cry through the cloudburst.

"Help!"

Kal was in the choppy river.

Aline rowed as fast as she could to the almost toppled canoe. She worried that someone had capsized in the river. She was stunned when she saw Kal holding onto the gunwale of his canoe with one hand. He was holding a piece of wood in his other hand.

"I've got this," he said.

"Didn't you just scream for help?" As Aline asked, the Thuumps turned up the dial on peril. Booming thunder shook the rainforest.

"There is a hole in the canoe. I hit a rock in the water because I row so fast."

"You mean because you don't pay attention? Do you need help or not?"

"I am trying to seal the leak. I need to lodge this piece of wood into the gash," Kal shouted over the gusts of wind.

"It's too late for that. If it doesn't work, your canoe will sink."

"I know that," Kal said gripping the side of his canoe. He tossed the piece of wood back in and Aline extended her oar to help Kal board her canoe. When she was distracted, the Thuumps made their move! Their number one goal is to steal our belongings through din and damage.

They stretched out their sour paws and
reached for Aline's map!

Princess Nahy-tro saw and wasn't about to let the soggy tater tots get away with their heist. Princess Nahy-tro lifted her shield, but at the same time Aline swatted at the spiky mist and when she did this - she knocked out two of the Thuumps! The other three dried meatballs went to help their friends and did not get their grimy mitts on Aline's map. For now, the sabotage of The Great Games was on hold.

"The storm is becoming stronger," Aline called as she began to row away.

"I can't leave my canoe. I'm about to win this race," Kal hooted like a Brown-Throated Three-Toed Sloth.

"This is no time for bragging, Kal! Here is a rope. Tie your canoe to it and help me row back," Aline raised her voice above the strong gales.

Well, misery loves company and those Thuumps were together again. They were on high alert. Thuumps do not like resolutions. So what did those troublesome rotten tomatoes do? They pulled out all their tricks. Just as the canoes were tied together and Aline and Kal began rowing back, the Thuumps created a cannonball of thunderous clomps and clumps. Sheets of rain fell down blocking Aline's view. Aline and Kal could not see that behind the sudden rainfall were the Thuumps. But, Princess Nahy-tro saw clearly.

If the duo had any chance against the troublemakers, Princess Nahy-tro would have to lend a hand.

Was there still time?

Chapter 10
Sailing Thunder

The Thuumps were trying to make
Kal's canoe so heavy that Aline would be
forced to cut it loose. The Thuumps
wanted both Aline and Kal to lose The
Great Games! They wanted them to blame
one another. Wind looped and curled
around Aline and Kal. Wind pounded the
canoes. The Thuumps wanted this
downpour to be Aline and Kal's downfall!

Princess Nahy-tro could see the hairy
legs and crusty toes of the Thuumps
sticking out of the rough, muddy, brown
river. *They really need to clip those toe
nails*, the princess thought. The princess
knew she would need to get the Thuumps
above water. She had the perfect shield!
With all her might, Princess Nahy-tro
pounded her Titan shield. The Titan
shield had magnetic power. And you know
those long toe nails of the Thuumps?
Well, they were made of rare metals from
the earth. Therefore, they were magnetic.
So, sure enough and one by one, the Titan
shield began to hoist each Thuump up
from the river. The Thuumps didn't want

to give in. They held on tight to one another, but the first Thuump's grip was glued to the canoe. Never fear, Princess Nahy-tro was stronger than those deceitful little chunks. Princess Nahy-tro sang a song of powerful rhymes that resonated in all the rainforest. Her song paralyzed the Thuumps. They stretched out like long, wiggly pieces of taffy as they were pulled upward by the Titan Shield.

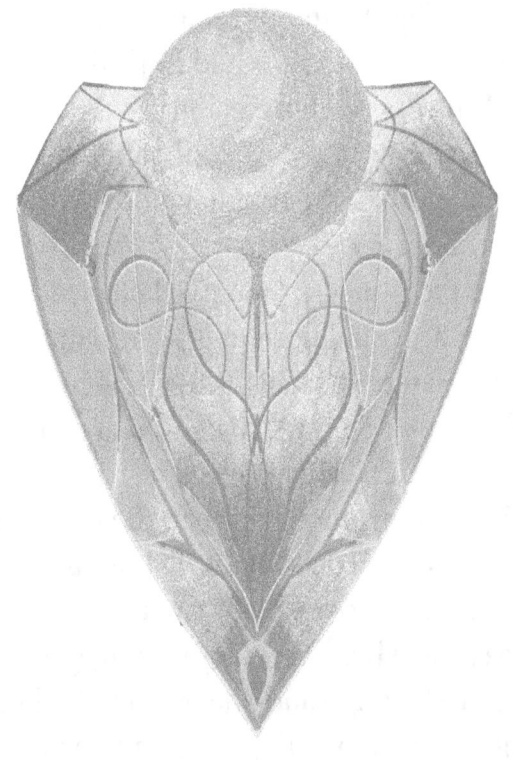

The wind twisted around Aline and Kal. Both of them had seen many storms. Neither of them recalled one this fierce. In one last strike of her Titan Shield, Princess Nahy-tro was able to loosen the tiny vicious clench of the last Thuump clinging to the canoe. Then in a nano second, she opened her tympanum and locked in the overripe rebellious spuds. The storms settled and Aline and Kal were free to race back. But, were they done with the five tasks?

Aline and Kal rowed as the distant thunder seemed to be saying goodbye. Other kids sped ahead. This was going to be a close race.

"I have to stop for honey!" Kal hollered.

"I needed to stop for bananas, but now we have to race back," Aline exclaimed.

"I can win this race if I can get a honeycomb!"

"The hives require patience, Kal. Plus, you can't travel far with a hole in your canoe."

"But I am supposed to be the winner!" Kal demanded.

"Kal, can you try to be happy that you are alive and well?"

"I deserve to win the crown!"

"Right now, it would be good news if we can make it back to shore safely."

Together they kneeled on the floor of the canoe and rowed as partners. This style of rowing made maneuvering the river a bit easier. They raced toward the finish line. When they saw the finish line, they cheered. They collected their baskets and hopped out.

"Here," Kal said as he tossed a bushel of bananas into Aline's last empty basket. "Thanks for helping me."

"Sure," Aline said surprised. Then she handed him a hunk of honeycomb.

"Kal,"

"Yeah?"

"Maybe you don't always have to win. Ever think that finishing the race is also great?"

"Of course not. Winning makes winners. That's how I see greatness."

Aline shook her head and tried to be polite, "Maybe you can try to see that having a chance to play the game makes us all a winner?"

"What do you mean?"

"I mean that it is wonderful to be great at a few things, but it sounds very stressful to try to be great at everything."

"I never thought of it like that."

"Other peoples' victories matter too. And Kal, it feels good to applaud them as well."

"Yeah, how would I do that?"

"Maybe don't steal their thunder every chance you get. Maybe save some of the spotlight for others once in a while?"

Grumble and growl

Rumble and roll

Thunder is the melody the Lightning Elves know

Be alert and listen

For a triumphant harmony on

your ears will glisten

All the children presented their baskets in the order they arrived back to shore. Aline and Kal watched as the winner was crowned with the most magnificent and bright headpiece.

The crown was full of rare blossoms. Everyone oohed and aahed.

Afterward, Kal and Aline told their parents the story of the wild storm and how they helped each other.

"Oh, Kal helped you row you back? Kal you saved her!" Kal's parents crowed.

"No, Aline rowed me back. Aline saved me."

And just like that the blaring horn in the Amazon was mute. All the parents were proud of their children for taking part in The Great Games.

After that day, Aline and Kal embarked on new adventures. From then on when the duo sailed, it was with the melody of

thunder in their hearts. This magical sound made Princess Nahy-tro proud as she looked on from her faraway land of Titan preparing for the adventure the next storm would bring.

This is what happens when you separate the Magical from the Tragical. You will embark on great adventures.

Dictionary Power = Superpowers

Try to build your superpowers!

☆ Find a new word in a story

☆ Write the new word on a clean page

☆ Say the new word *Out Loud*

☆ Take a Guess. How many different definitions do you think that word has?

☆ Write your guess next to the new word

☆ Look up the new word in the dictionary

☆ Say the new word again *Out Loud*

☆ Read each of the definitions

☆ Count the # of definitions

☆ Compare. How close did you get to the correct # of definitions?

☆ Try to use a new word a day

Did you know that all the words in the world belong to you? New vocabulary used in positive ways builds your **Power of Sound**!

Readers Make Thinkers!

A Spot The Differences Learning Activity

→

Can you make a list of the many animals you see in each illustration?

How many were included in the story?

Can you make a list of the sounds you would hear if you stepped into the illustration?

What would you feel if you touched a banana tree or the river, a plant or one of the animals?

Write down the colors that you see,

Can you trace the macaw on Page 4 on a new piece of paper?

On colorful strips of paper, write descriptions from your lists. Only add 1 item per strip.

Can you glue the strips to your macaw to make feathers? The more descriptions you have, the fluffier your macaw will be.

Example Strip

Find other books from the Author including:

The Thunder Maker and
The Adventure of the Apology Letter

The Author loves hearing from readers. Follow
for updates on Book Events and new books!

@RothmanEditions